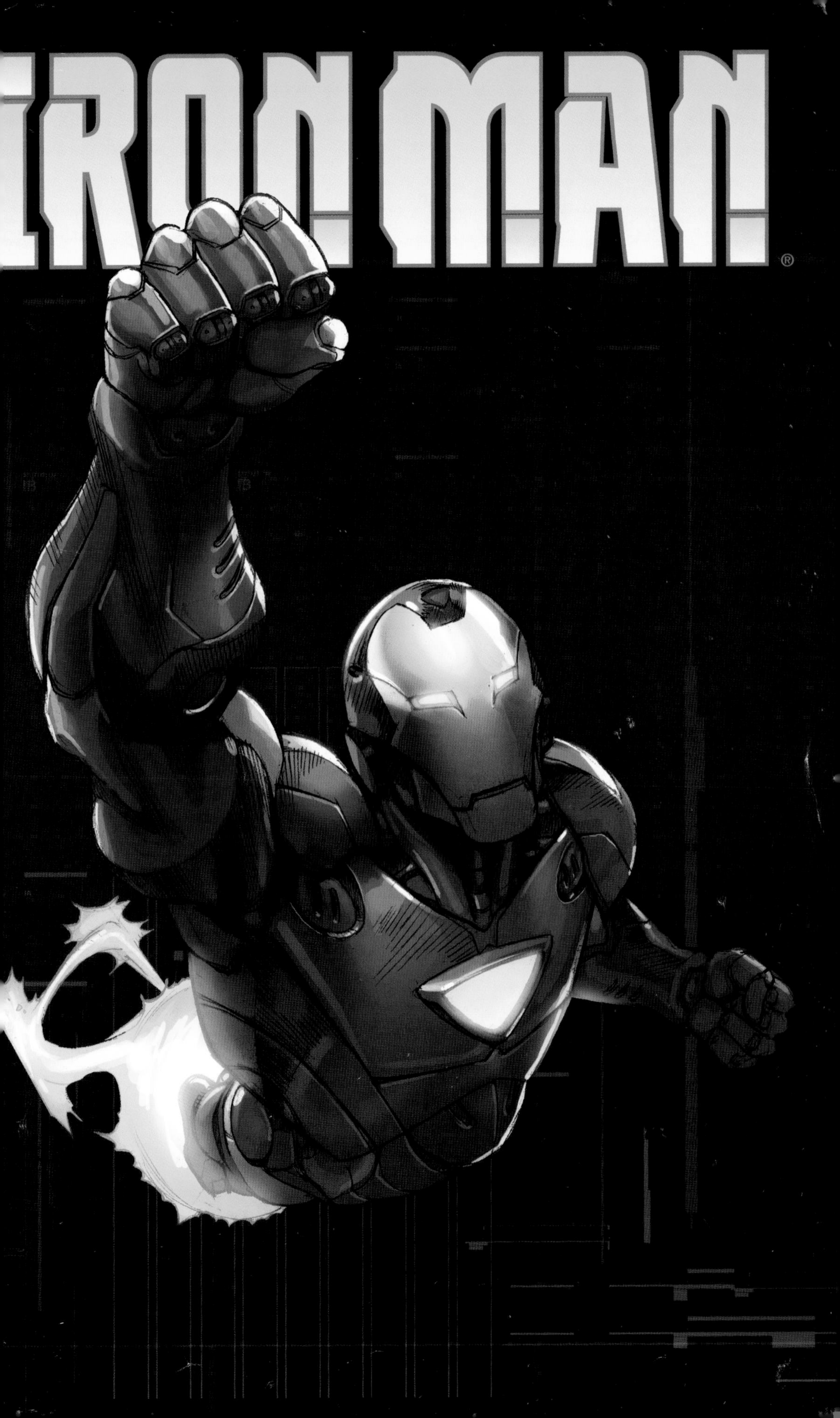
IRON MAN®

VISIT US AT
www.abdopublishing.com

Reinforced library bound edition published in 2011 by Spotlight, a division of the ABDO Group, 8000 West 78th Street, Edina, Minnesota 55439. Spotlight produces high-quality reinforced library bound editions for schools and libraries. Published by agreement with Marvel Characters, Inc.

Printed in the United States of America, Melrose Park, Illinois.
042010
092010
♻ This book contains at least 10% recycled material.

Library of Congress Cataloging-in-Publication Data

Van Lente, Fred.
 Web of lies / story, Fred Van Lente ; art, Graham Nolan.
    p. cm. -- (Iron Man)
 "Marvel."
 ISBN 978-1-59961-774-9
 1. Graphic novels. [1. Graphic novels. 2. Superheroes--Fiction.] I. Nolan, Graham, ill. II. Title.
PZ7.7.V26Web 2010
 741.5'973--dc22
                        2009052839

All Spotlight books have reinforced library bindings and
are manufactured in the United States of America.

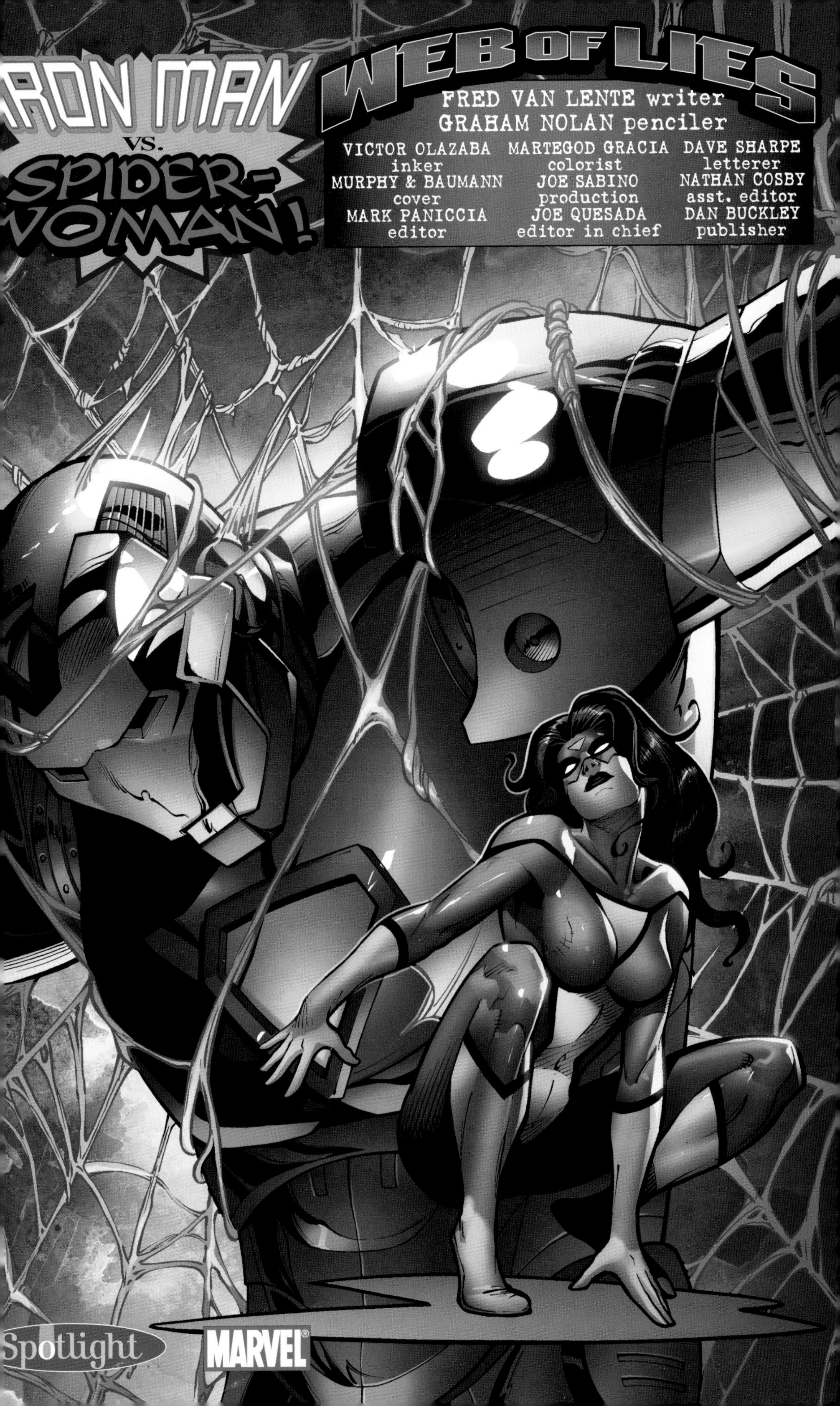

IRON MAN VS. SPIDER-WOMAN!
WEB OF LIES
FRED VAN LENTE writer
GRAHAM NOLAN penciler
VICTOR OLAZABA inker
MARTEGOD GRACIA colorist
DAVE SHARPE letterer
MURPHY & BAUMANN cover
JOE SABINO production
NATHAN COSBY asst. editor
MARK PANICCIA editor
JOE QUESADA editor in chief
DAN BUCKLEY publisher
Spotlight
MARVEL

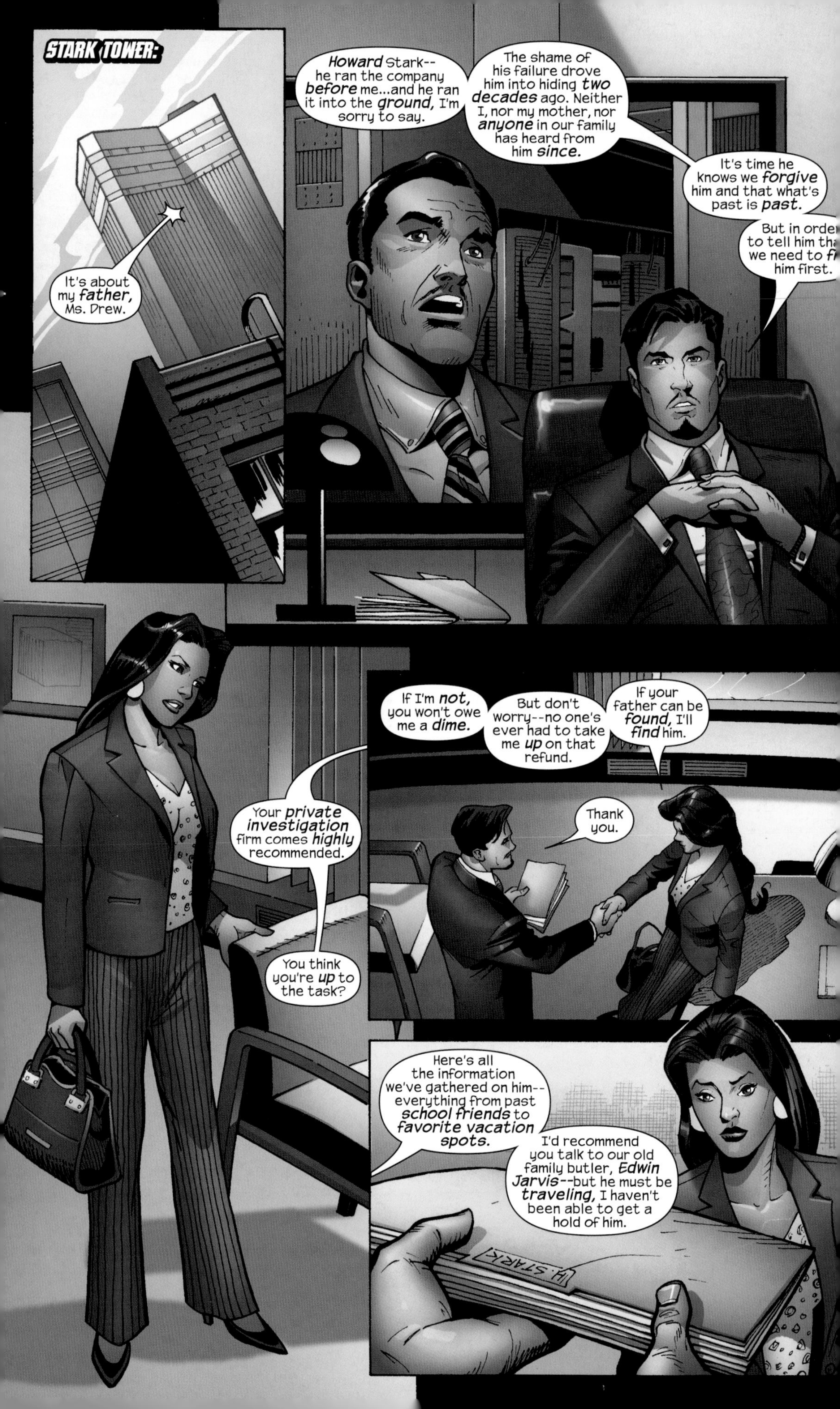
STARK TOWER:
It's about my father, Ms. Drew.
Howard Stark--he ran the company before me...and he ran it into the ground, I'm sorry to say.
The shame of his failure drove him into hiding two decades ago. Neither I, nor my mother, nor anyone in our family has heard from him since.
It's time he knows we forgive him and that what's past is past.
But in orde to tell him tha we need to fi him first.
Your private investigation firm comes highly recommended.
You think you're up to the task?
If your father can be found, I'll find him.
But don't worry--no one's ever had to take me up on that refund.
If I'm not, you won't owe me a dime.
Thank you.
Here's all the information we've gathered on him--everything from past school friends to favorite vacation spots.
I'd recommend you talk to our old family butler, Edwin Jarvis--but he must be traveling, I haven't been able to get a hold of him.
H. STARK

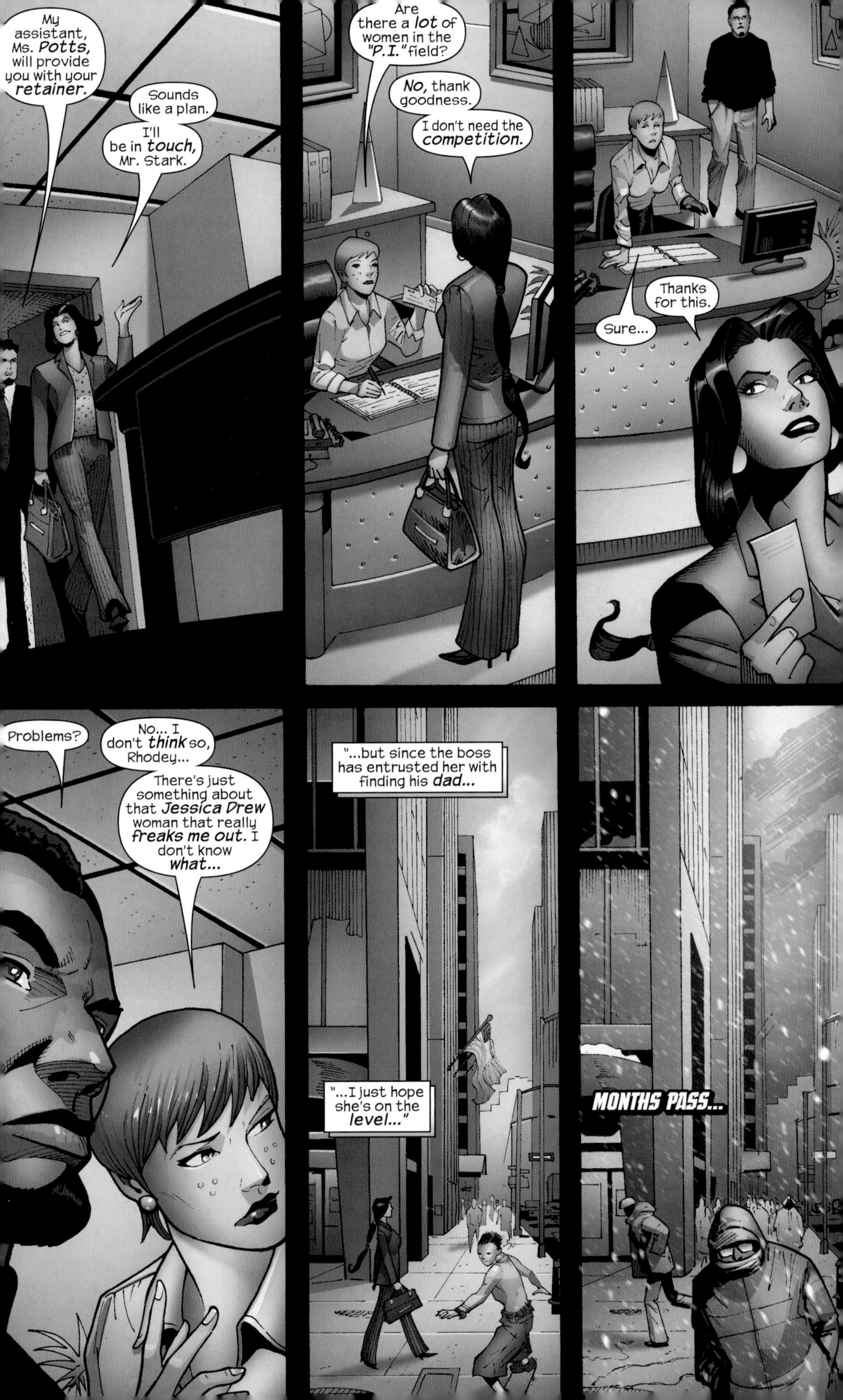

My assistant, Ms. Potts, will provide you with your retainer.
Sounds like a plan.
I'll be in touch, Mr. Stark.
Are there a lot of women in the "P.I." field?
No, thank goodness.
I don't need the competition.
Thanks for this.
Sure...
Problems?
No... I don't think so, Rhodey...
There's just something about that Jessica Drew woman that really freaks me out. I don't know what...
"...but since the boss has entrusted her with finding his dad...
"...I just hope she's on the level..."
MONTHS PASS...

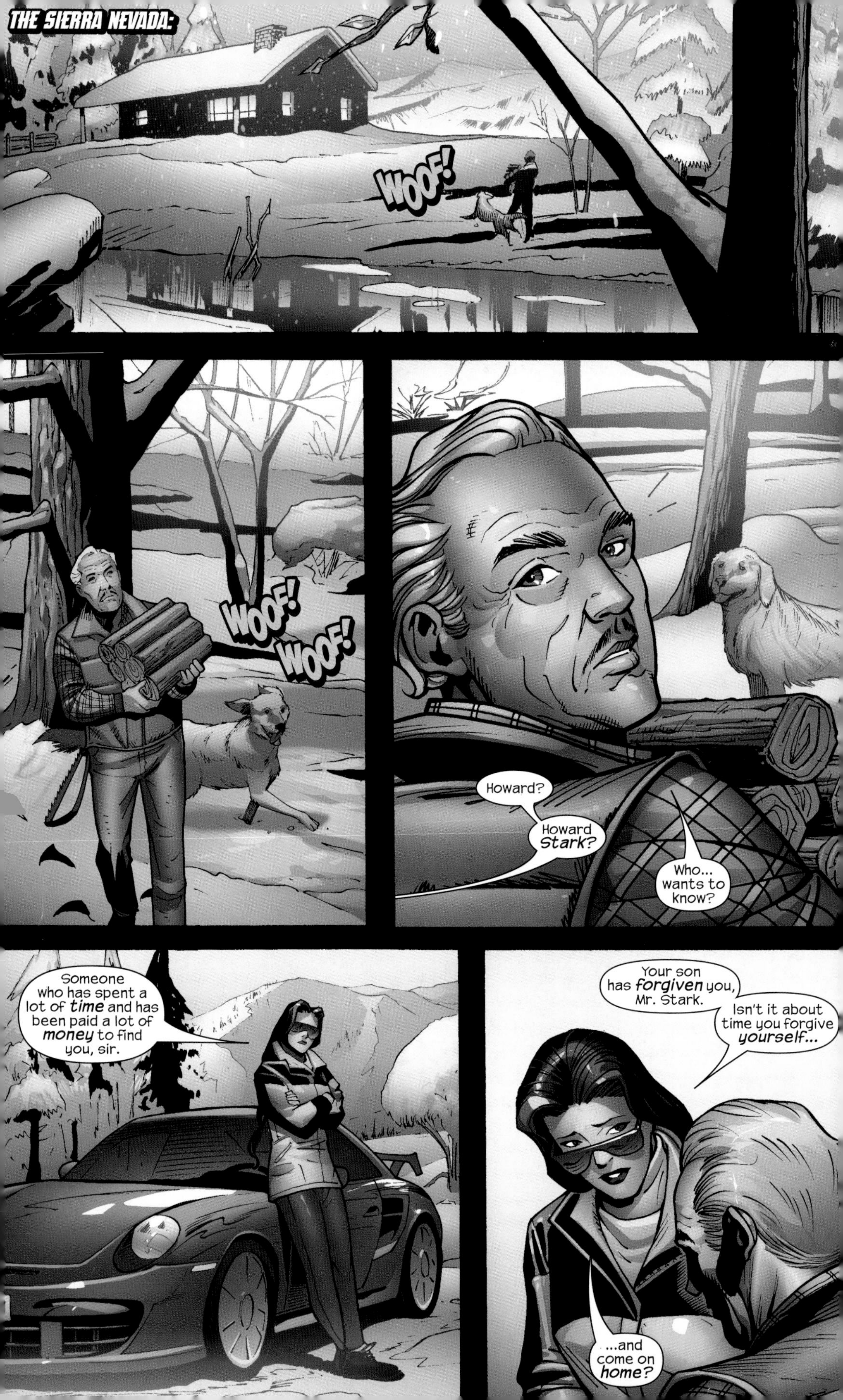
THE SIERRA NEVADA:
WOOF!
WOOF!
WOOF!
Howard?
Howard Stark?
Who... wants to know?
Someone who has spent a lot of time and has been paid a lot of money to find you, sir.
Your son has forgiven you, Mr. Stark.
Isn't it about time you forgive yourself...
...and come on home?

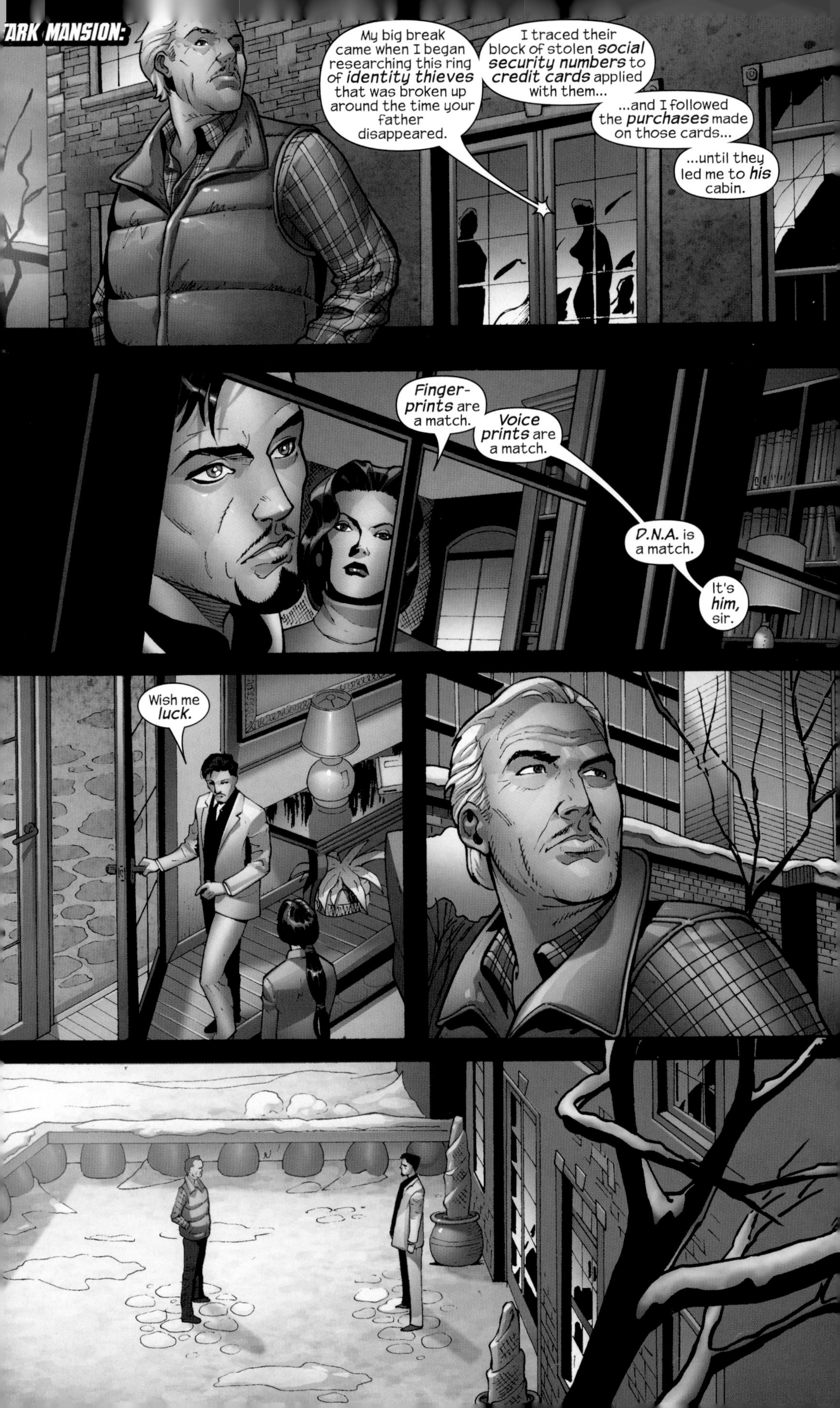
ARK MANSION:
My big break came when I began researching this ring of identity thieves that was broken up around the time your father disappeared.
I traced their block of stolen social security numbers to credit cards applied with them...
...and I followed the purchases made on those cards...
...until they led me to his cabin.
Finger-prints are a match.
Voice prints are a match.
D.N.A. is a match.
It's him, sir.
Wish me luck.

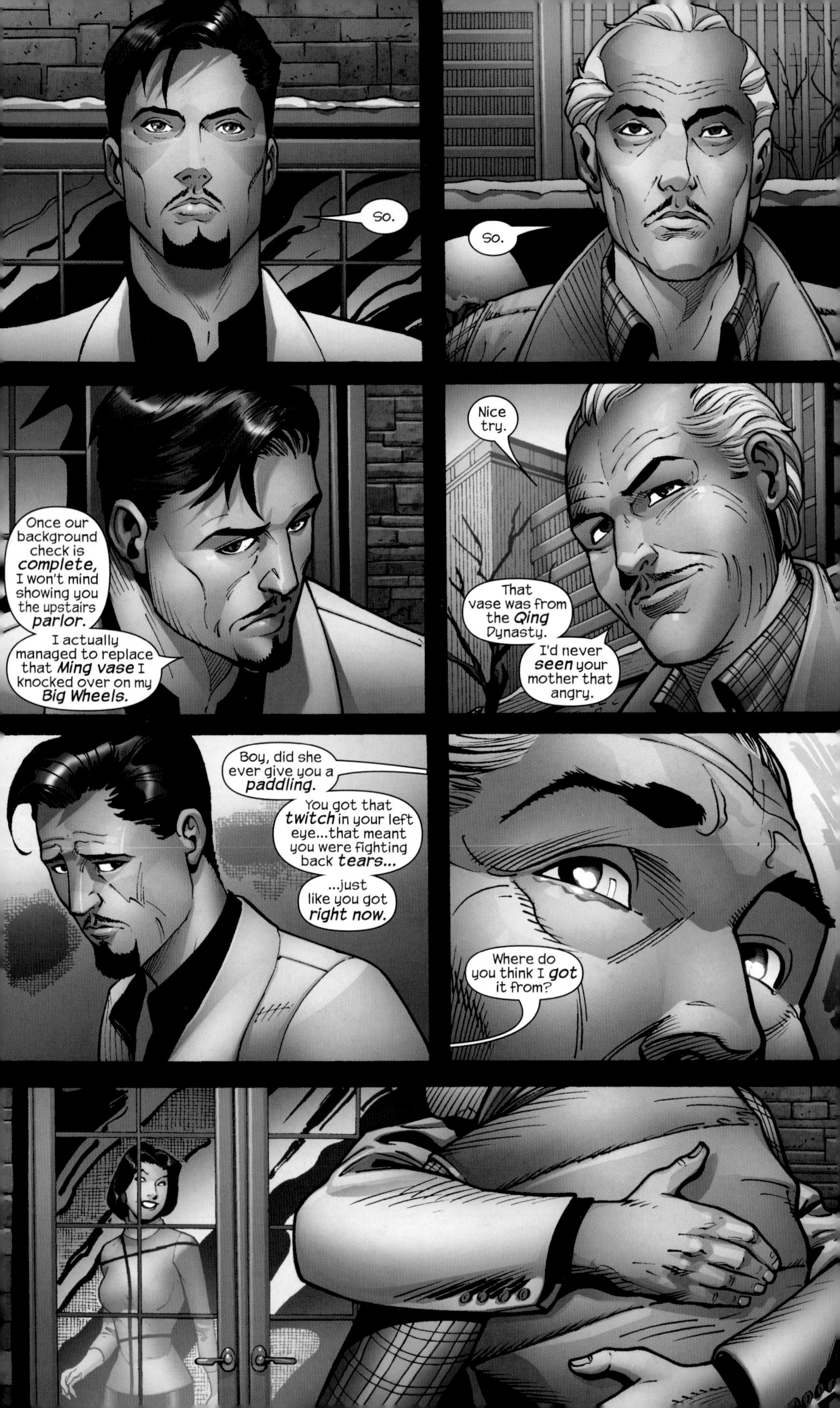
So.
So.
Once our background check is complete, I won't mind showing you the upstairs parlor.
I actually managed to replace that Ming vase I knocked over on my Big Wheels.
Nice try.
That vase was from the Qing Dynasty.
I'd never seen your mother that angry.
Boy, did she ever give you a paddling.
You got that twitch in your left eye...that meant you were fighting back tears...
...just like you got right now.
Where do you think I got it from?

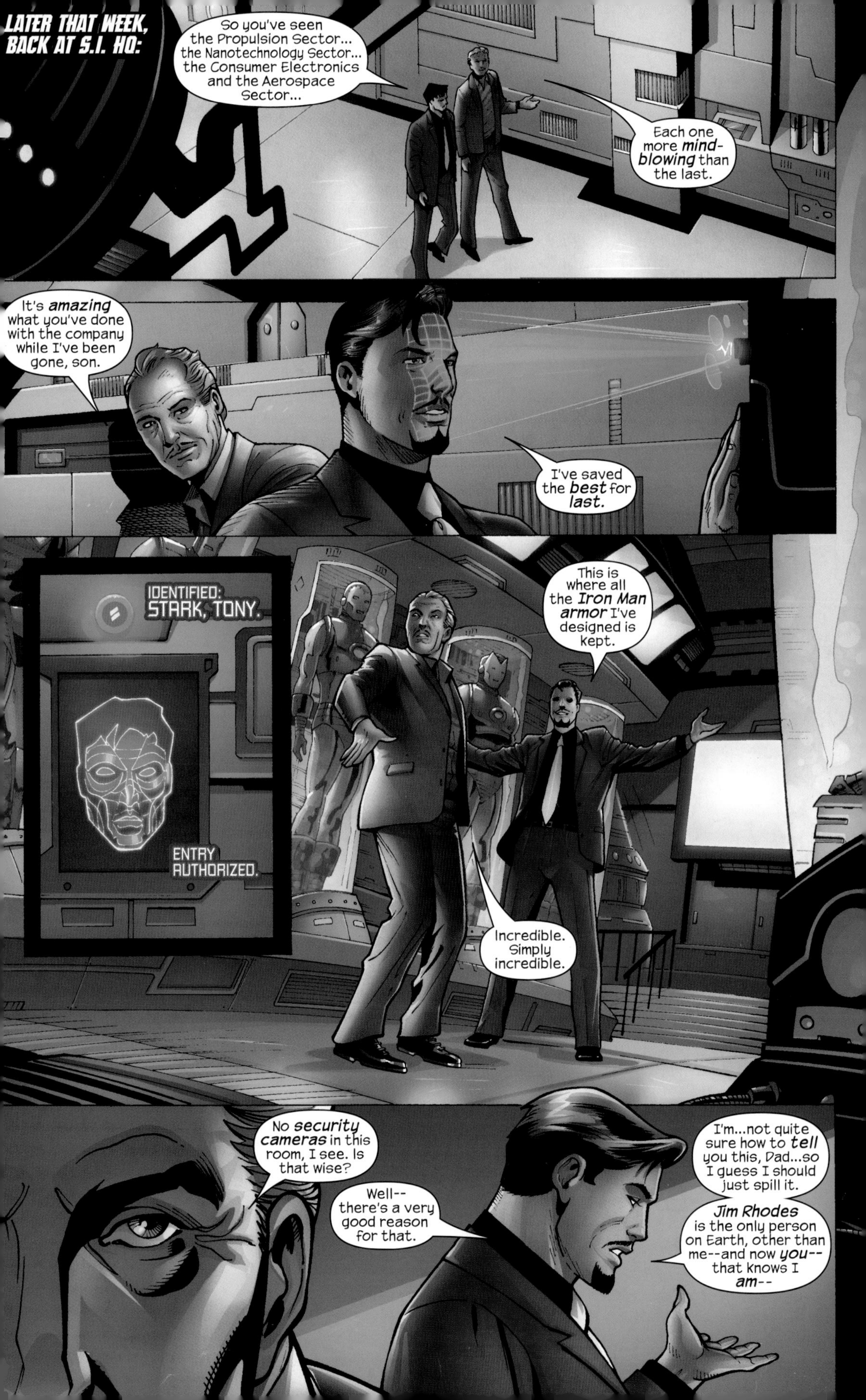
LATER THAT WEEK, BACK AT S.I. HQ:
So you've seen the Propulsion Sector... the Nanotechnology Sector... the Consumer Electronics and the Aerospace Sector...
Each one more *mind-blowing* than the last.
It's *amazing* what you've done with the company while I've been gone, son.
I've saved the *best* for *last.*
IDENTIFIED: STARK, TONY.
ENTRY AUTHORIZED.
This is where all the *Iron Man armor* I've designed is kept.
Incredible. Simply incredible.
No *security cameras* in this room, I see. Is that wise?
Well-- there's a very good reason for that.
I'm...not quite sure how to *tell* you this, Dad...so I guess I should just spill it.
Jim Rhodes is the only person on Earth, other than me--and now *you*-- that knows I *am*--

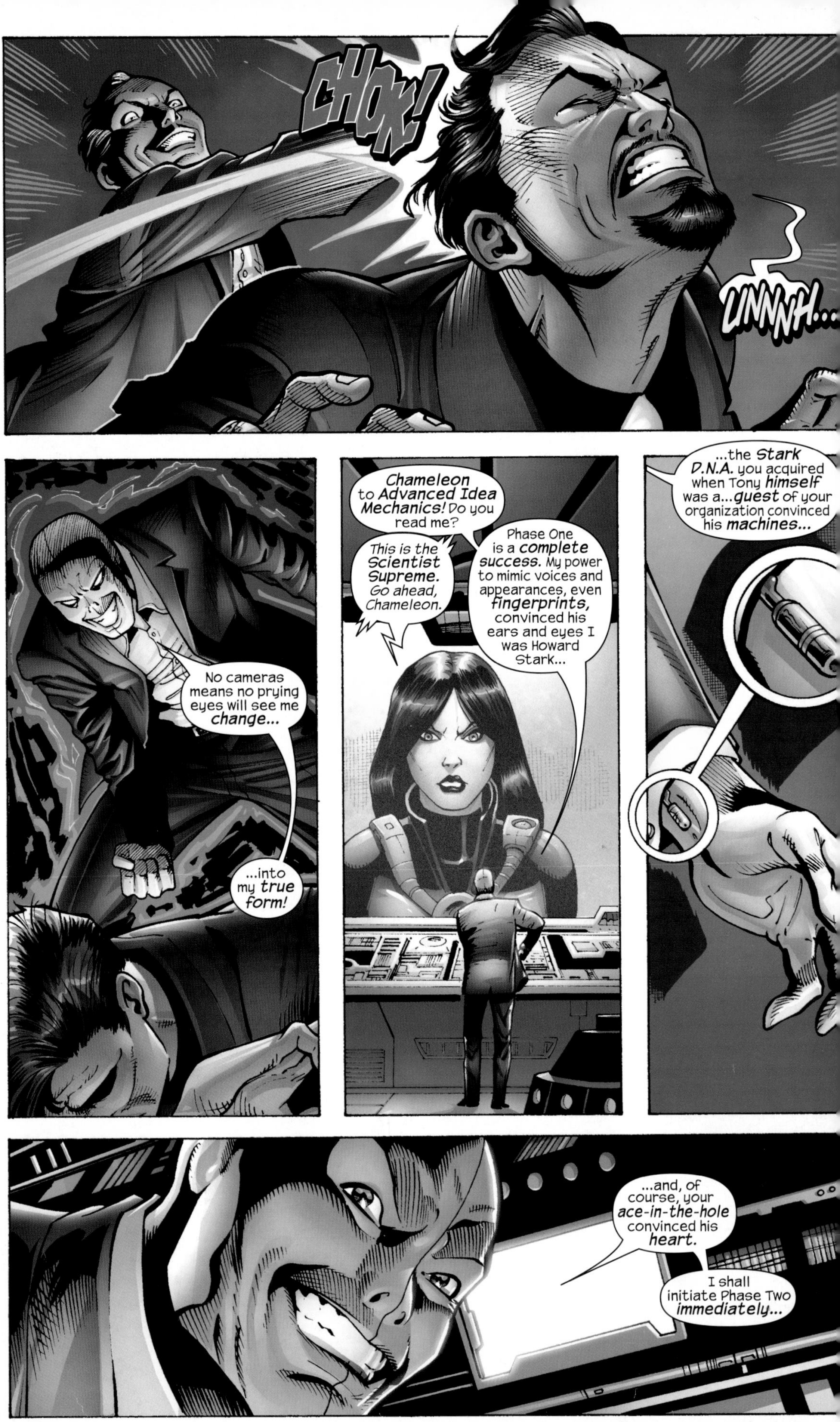
CHOK!
UNNNH...
No cameras means no prying eyes will see me change...
...into my true form!
Chameleon to Advanced Idea Mechanics! Do you read me?
This is the Scientist Supreme. Go ahead, Chameleon.
Phase One is a complete success. My power to mimic voices and appearances, even fingerprints, convinced his ears and eyes I was Howard Stark...
...the Stark D.N.A. you acquired when Tony himself was a...guest of your organization convinced his machines...
...and, of course, your ace-in-the-hole convinced his heart.
I shall initiate Phase Two immediately...

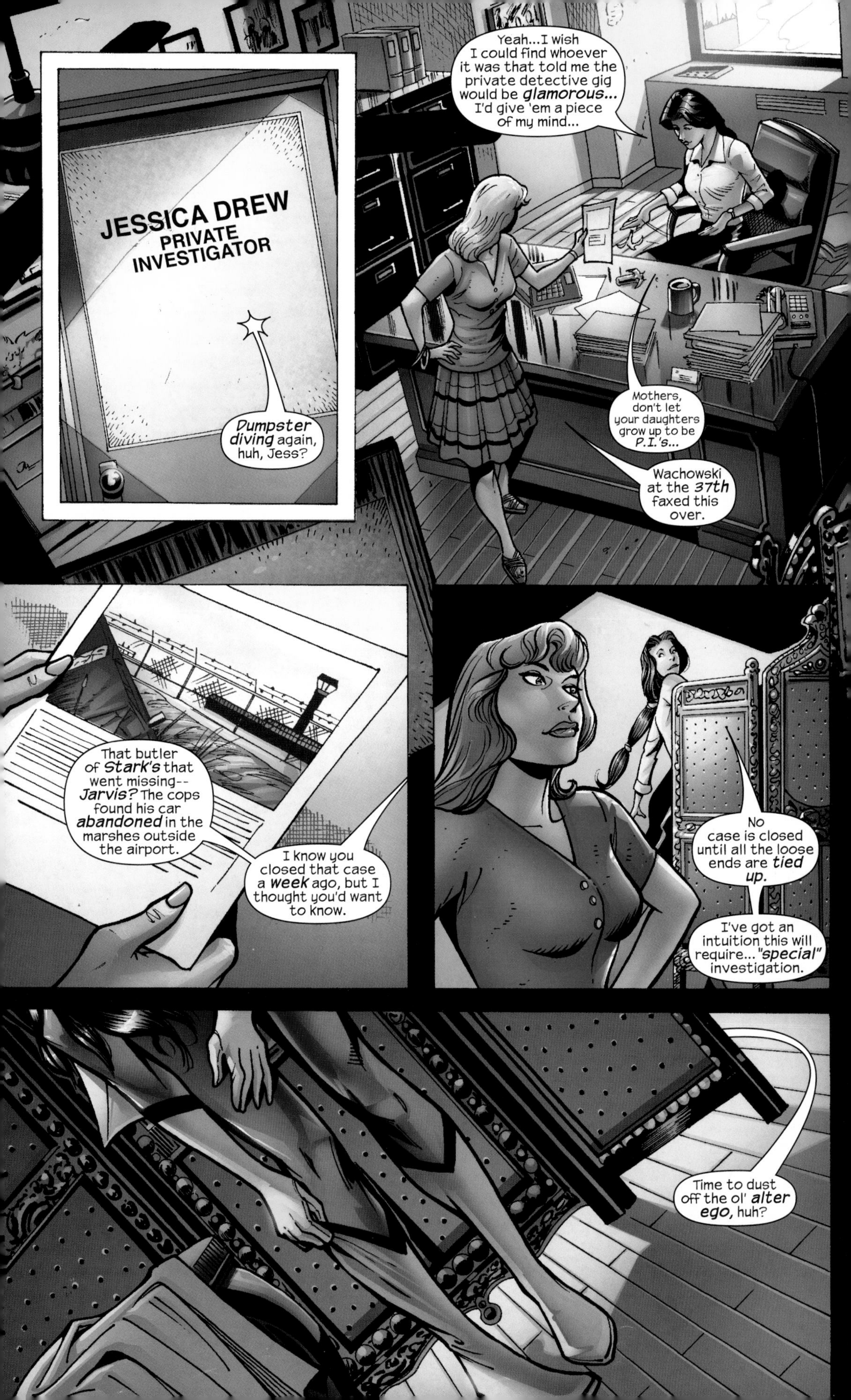

JESSICA DREW
PRIVATE INVESTIGATOR
Dumpster diving again, huh, Jess?
Yeah...I wish I could find whoever it was that told me the private detective gig would be glamorous... I'd give 'em a piece of my mind...
Mothers, don't let your daughters grow up to be P.I.'s...
Wachowski at the 37th faxed this over.
That butler of Stark's that went missing-- Jarvis? The cops found his car abandoned in the marshes outside the airport.
I know you closed that case a week ago, but I thought you'd want to know.
No case is closed until all the loose ends are tied up.
I've got an intuition this will require... "special" investigation.
Time to dust off the ol' alter ego, huh?

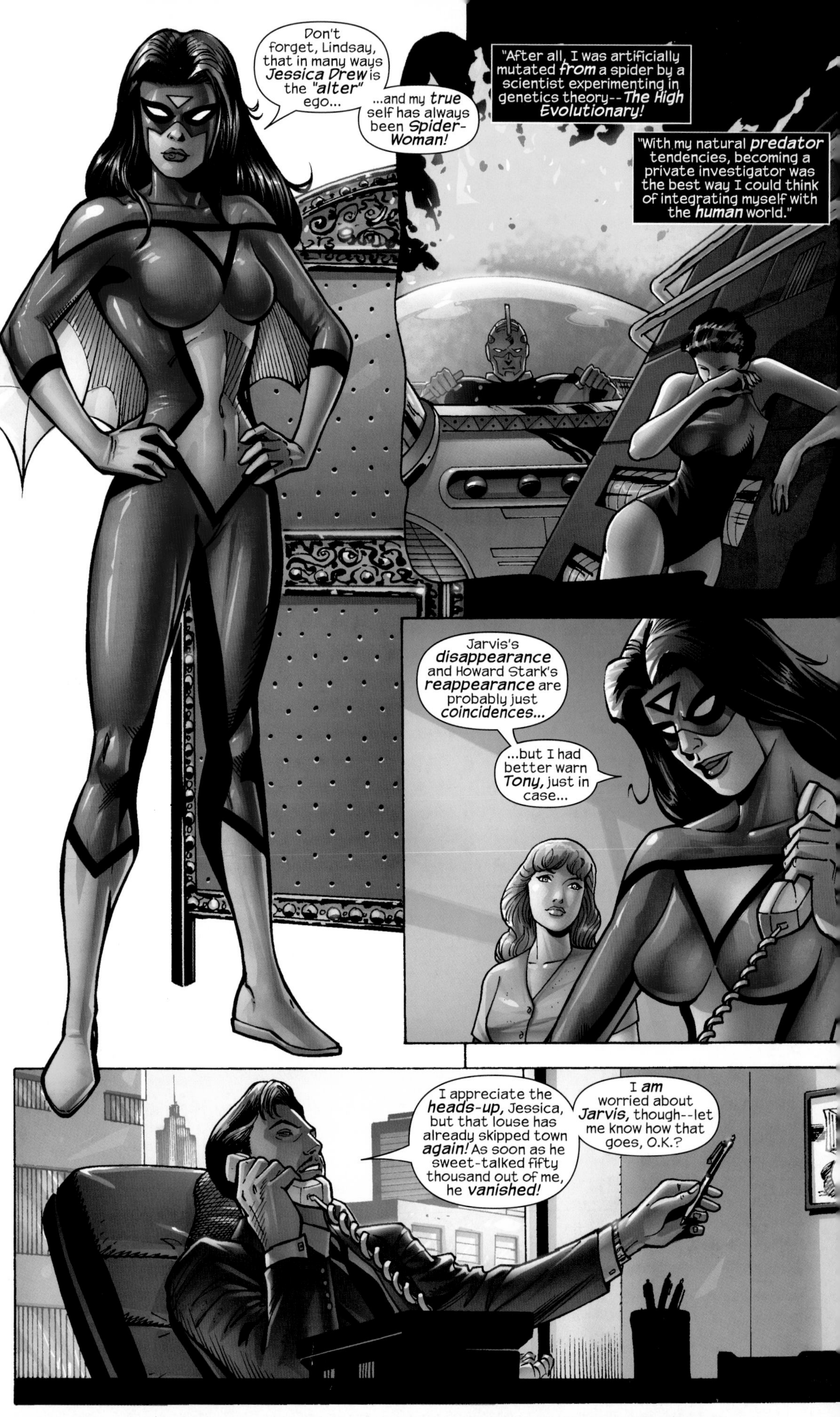
Don't forget, Lindsay, that in many ways Jessica Drew is the "alter" ego...
...and my true self has always been Spider-Woman!
"After all, I was artificially mutated from a spider by a scientist experimenting in genetics theory--The High Evolutionary!
"With my natural predator tendencies, becoming a private investigator was the best way I could think of integrating myself with the human world."
Jarvis's disappearance and Howard Stark's reappearance are probably just coincidences...
...but I had better warn Tony, just in case...
I appreciate the heads-up, Jessica, but that louse has already skipped town again! As soon as he sweet-talked fifty thousand out of me, he vanished!
I am worried about Jarvis, though--let me know how that goes, O.K.?

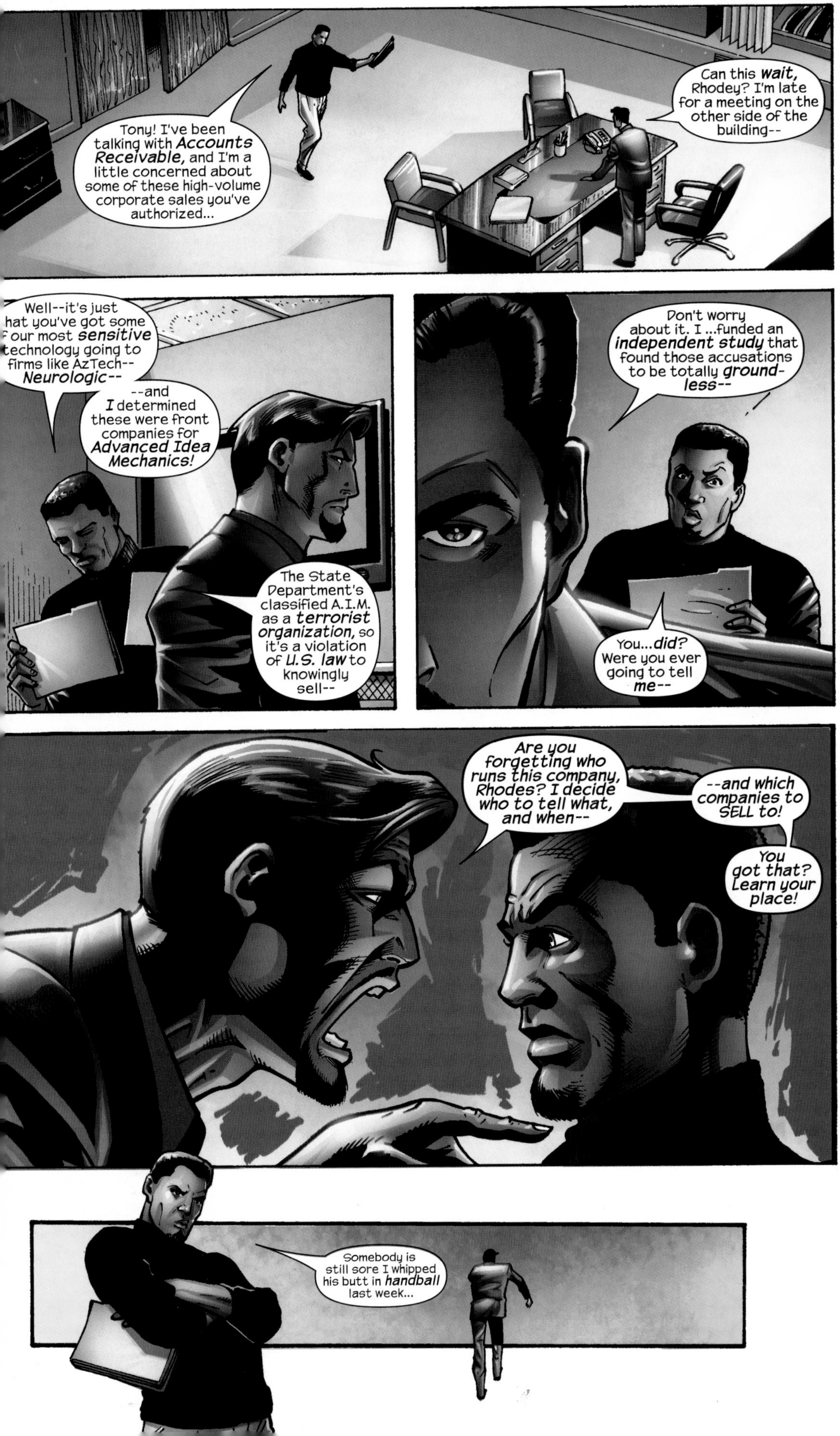

Tony! I've been talking with *Accounts Receivable,* and I'm a little concerned about some of these high-volume corporate sales you've authorized...
Can this *wait,* Rhodey? I'm late for a meeting on the other side of the building--
Well--it's just hat you've got some f our most *sensitive* technology going to firms like AzTech-- *Neurologic--*
--and *I* determined these were front companies for *Advanced Idea Mechanics!*
The State Department's classified A.I.M. as a *terrorist organization,* so it's a violation of *U.S. law* to knowingly sell--
Don't worry about it. I ...funded an *independent study* that found those accusations to be totally *ground-less--*
You...*did?* Were you ever going to tell *me--*
Are you forgetting who runs this company, Rhodes? I decide who to tell what, and when--
--and which companies to SELL to!
You got that? Learn your place!
Somebody is still sore I whipped his butt in *handball* last week...

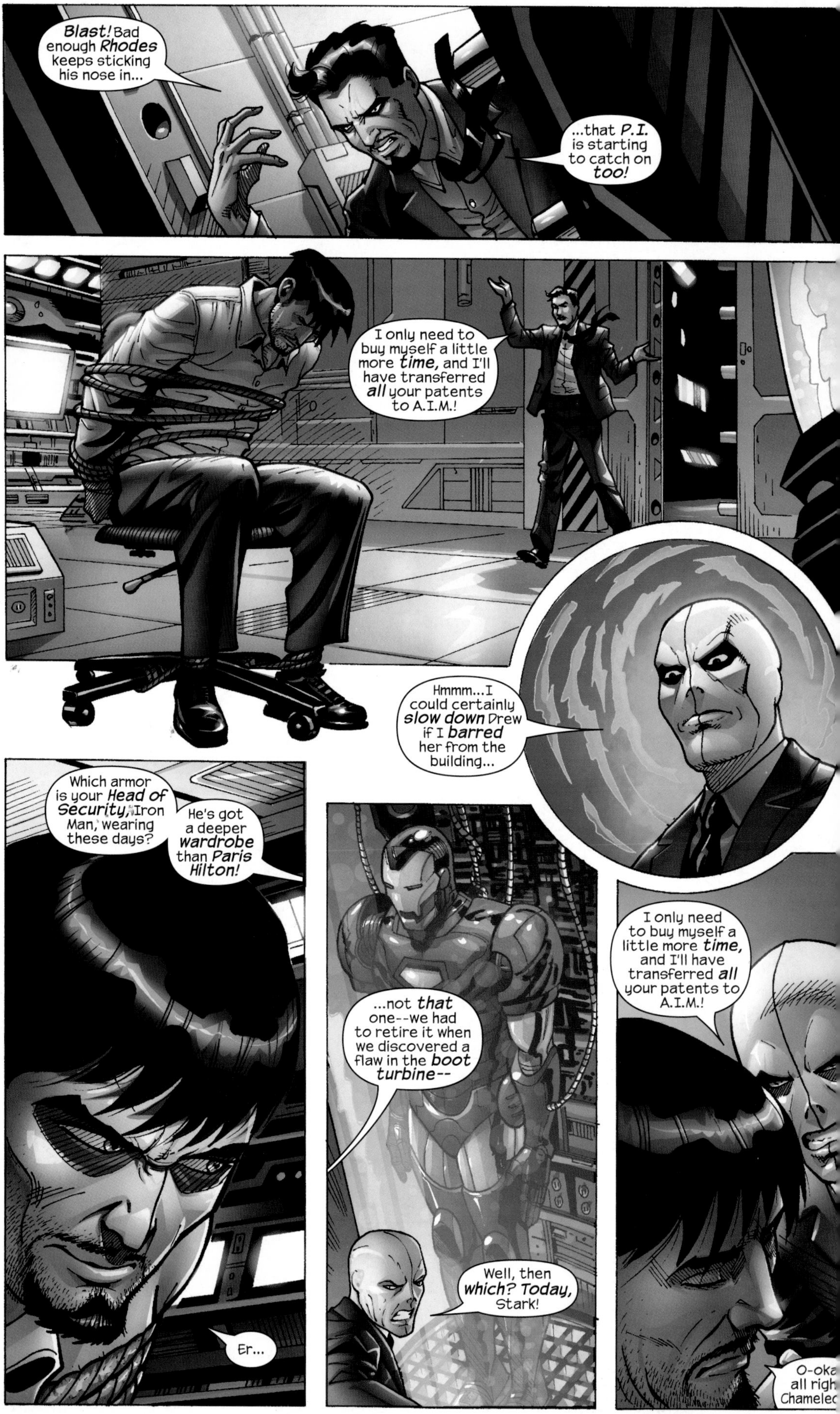

Blast! Bad enough Rhodes keeps sticking his nose in...
...that P.I. is starting to catch on too!
I only need to buy myself a little more time, and I'll have transferred all your patents to A.I.M.!
Hmmm...I could certainly slow down Drew if I barred her from the building...
Which armor is your Head of Security, Iron Man, wearing these days?
He's got a deeper wardrobe than Paris Hilton!
Er...
...not that one--we had to retire it when we discovered a flaw in the boot turbine--
Well, then which? Today, Stark!
I only need to buy myself a little more time, and I'll have transferred all your patents to A.I.M.!

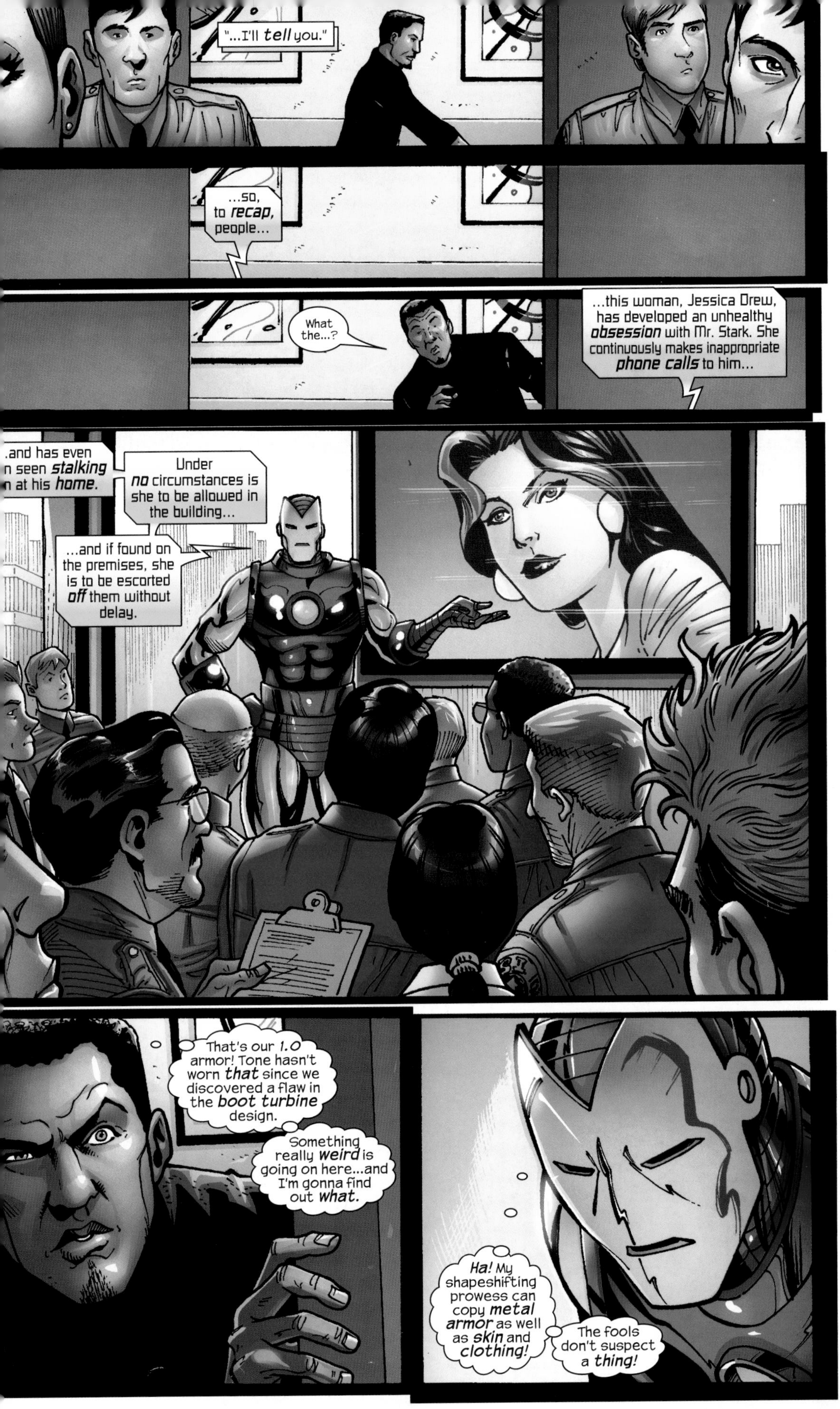
"...I'll tell you."
...so, to recap, people...
What the...?
...this woman, Jessica Drew, has developed an unhealthy obsession with Mr. Stark. She continuously makes inappropriate phone calls to him...
.and has even
n seen stalking
n at his home.
Under no circumstances is she to be allowed in the building...
...and if found on the premises, she is to be escorted off them without delay.
That's our 1.0 armor! Tone hasn't worn that since we discovered a flaw in the boot turbine design.
Something really weird is going on here...and I'm gonna find out what.
Ha! My shapeshifting prowess can copy metal armor as well as skin and clothing!
The fools don't suspect a thing!

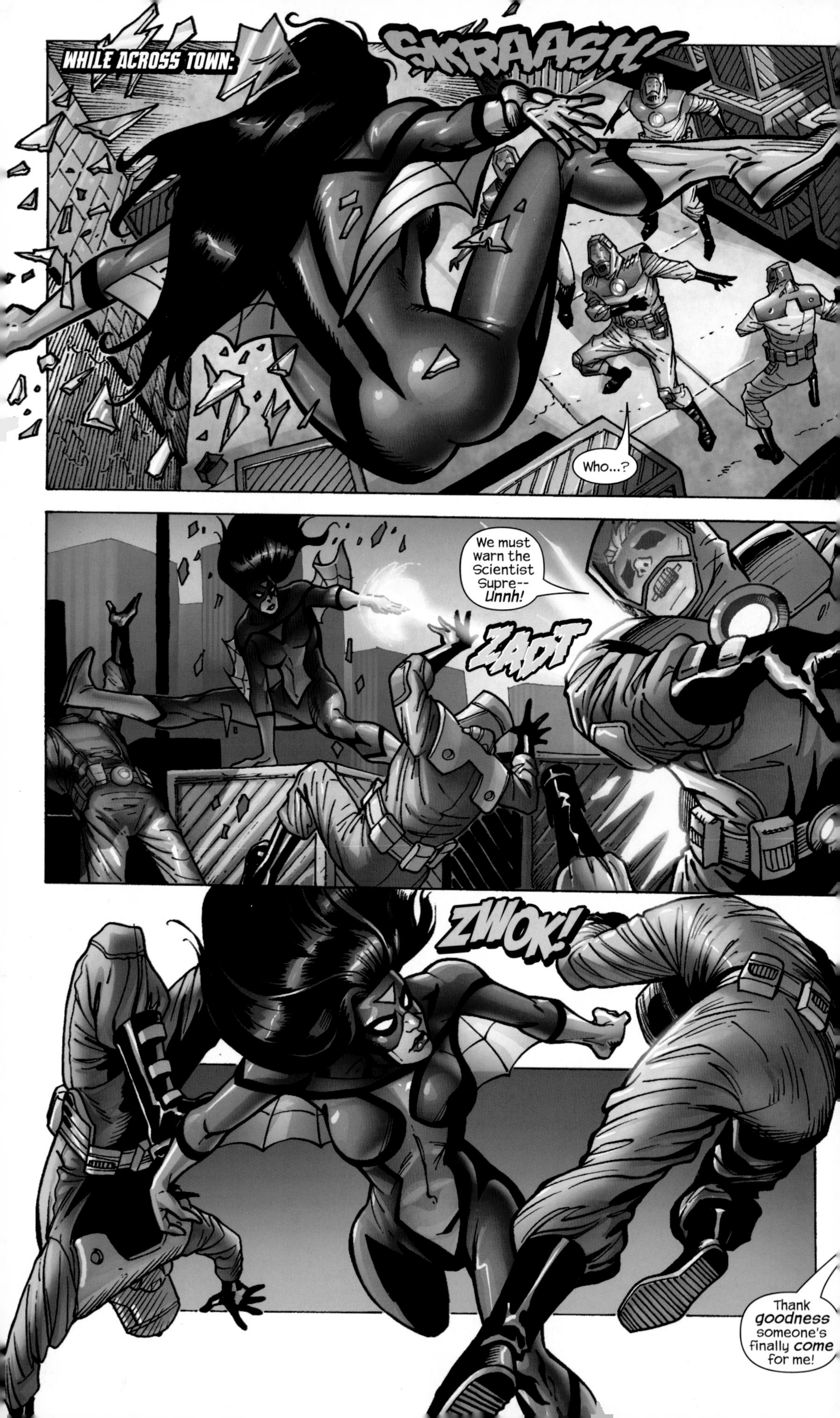
WHILE ACROSS TOWN:
SKRAASH!
Who...?
We must warn the Scientist Supre-- Unnh!
ZADT
ZWOK!
Thank goodness someone's finally come for me!

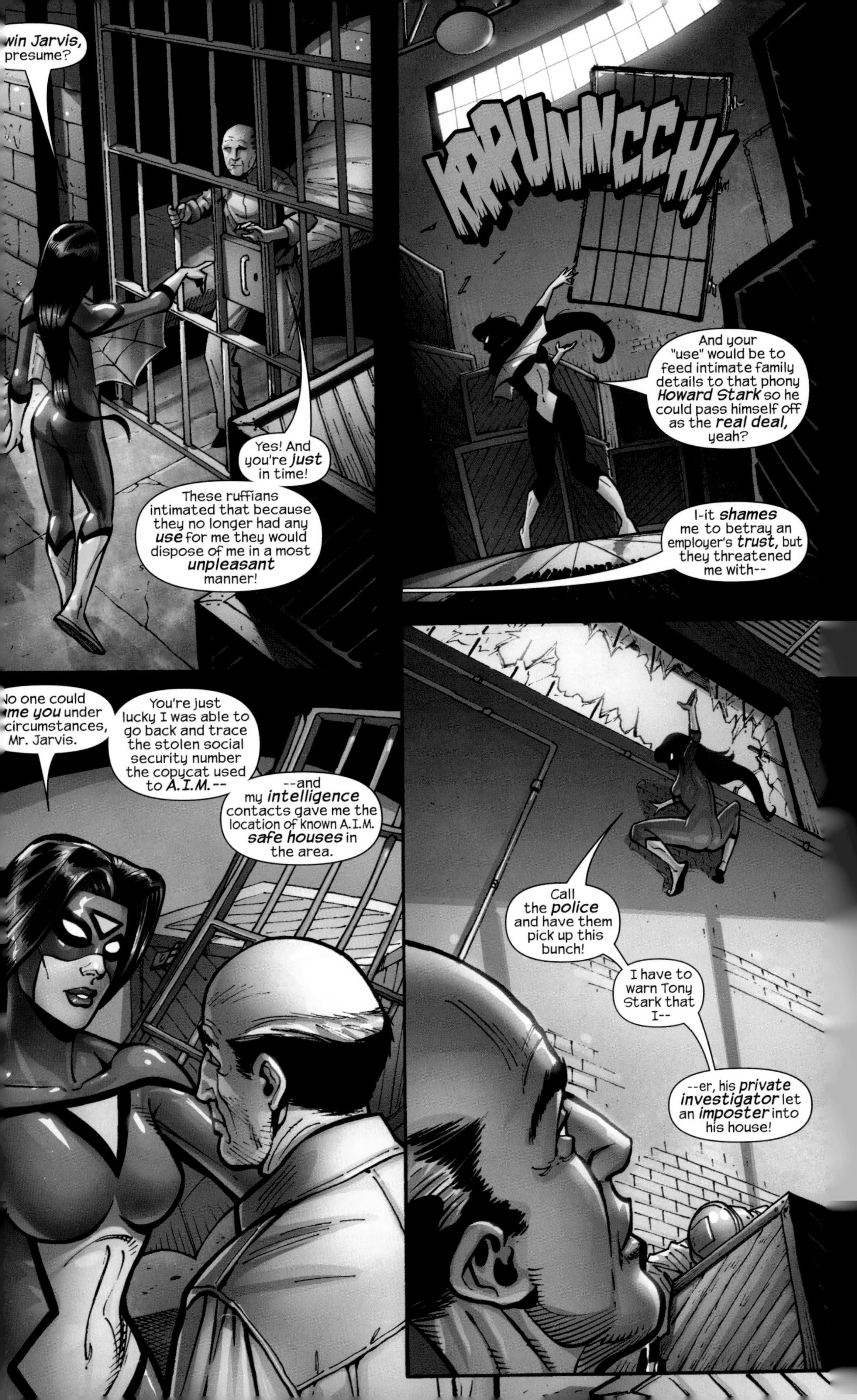

win Jarvis, presume?
Yes! And you're *just* in time!
These ruffians intimated that because they no longer had any *use* for me they would dispose of me in a most *unpleasant* manner!
KRRUNNCCH!
And your "use" would be to feed intimate family details to that phony *Howard Stark* so he could pass himself off as the *real deal,* yeah?
I-it *shames* me to betray an employer's *trust,* but they threatened me with--
No one could ame you under circumstances, Mr. Jarvis.
You're just lucky I was able to go back and trace the stolen social security number the copycat used to *A.I.M.*--
--and my *intelligence* contacts gave me the location of known A.I.M. *safe houses* in the area.
Call the *police* and have them pick up this bunch!
I have to warn Tony Stark that I--
--er, his *private investigator* let an *imposter* into his house!

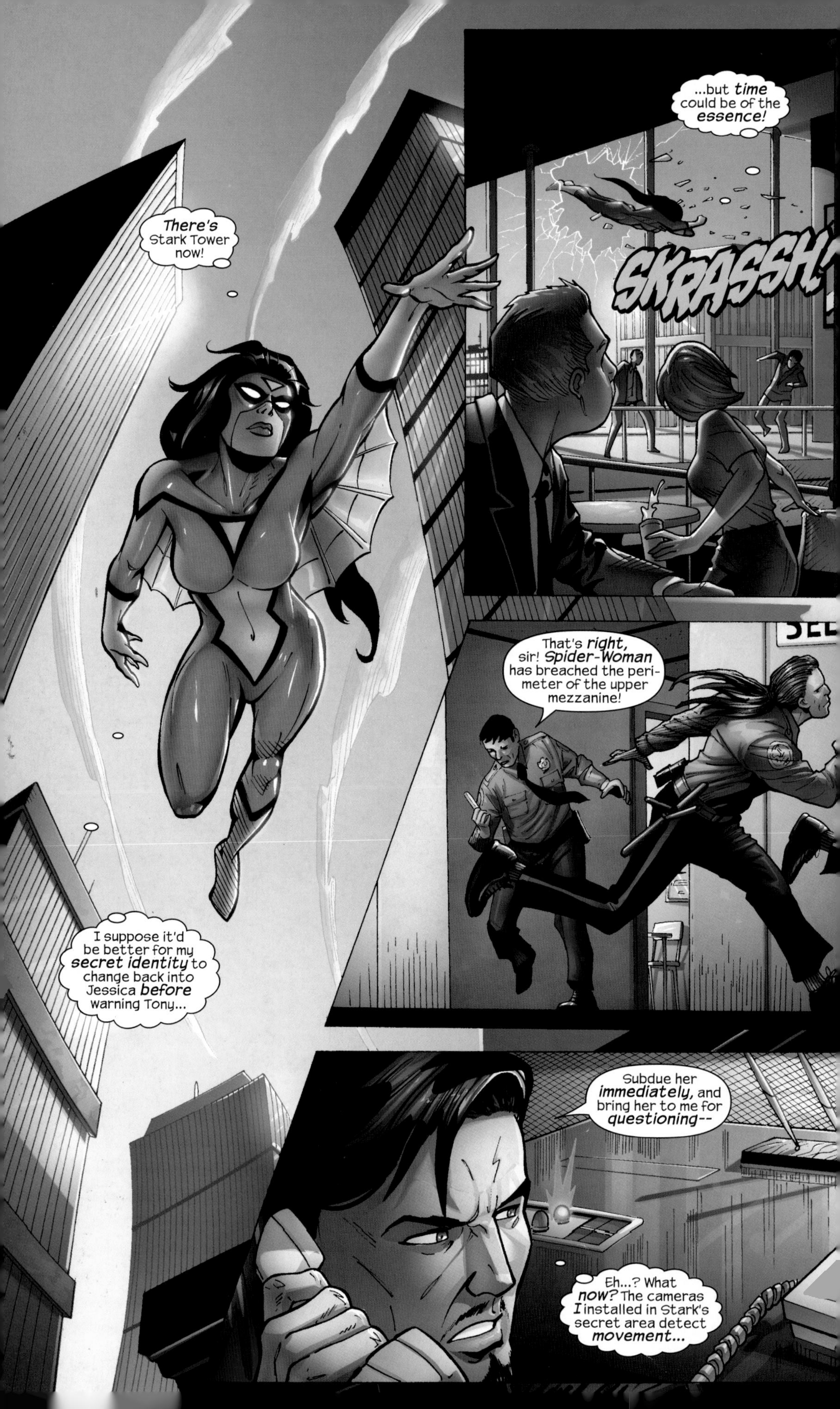
There's Stark Tower now!
I suppose it'd be better for my secret identity to change back into Jessica before warning Tony...
...but time could be of the essence!
SKRASSH
That's right, sir! Spider-Woman has breached the perimeter of the upper mezzanine!
Subdue her immediately, and bring her to me for questioning--
Eh...? What now? The cameras I installed in Stark's secret area detect movement...

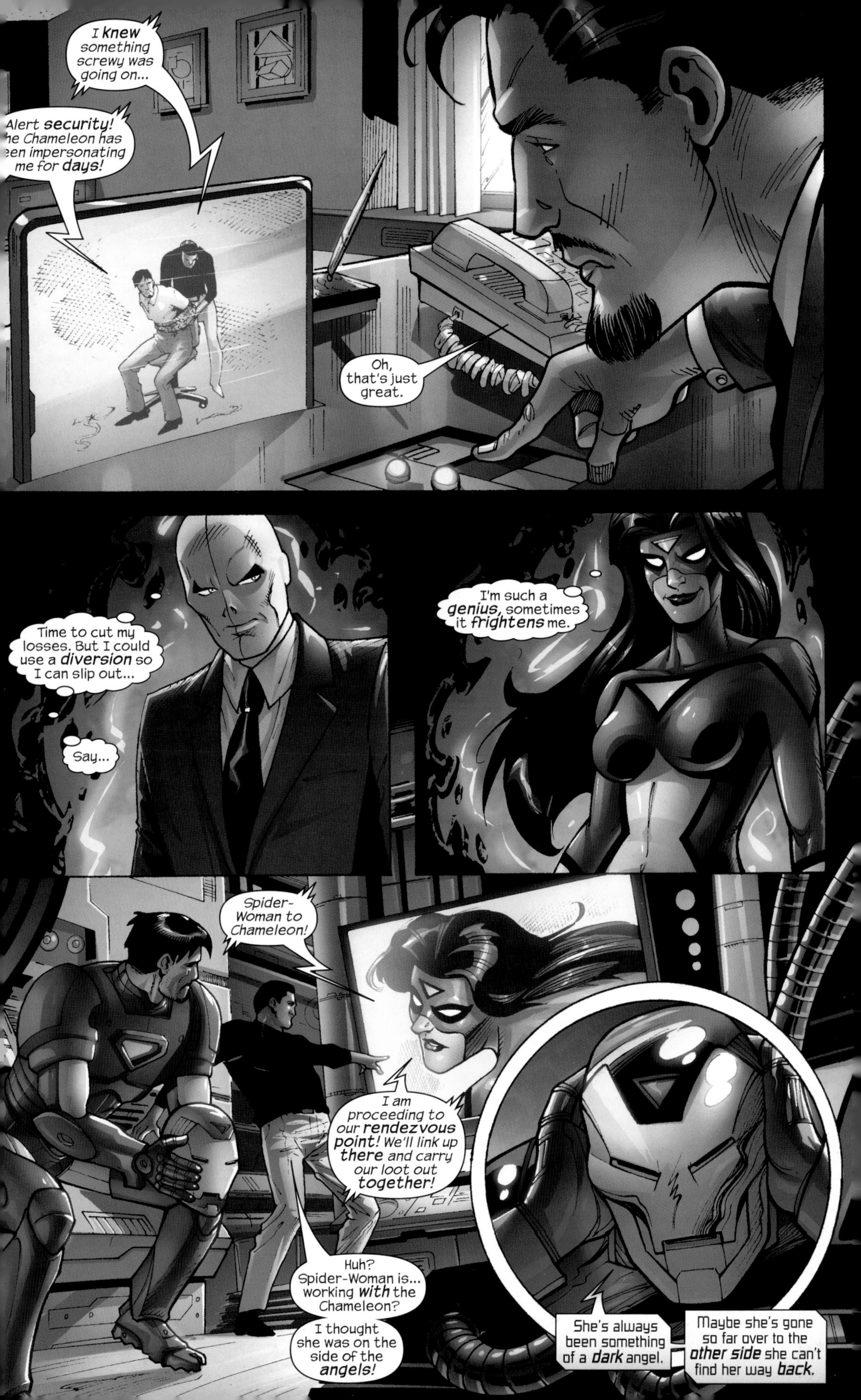
I knew something screwy was going on...
Alert security! he Chameleon has een impersonating me for days!
Oh, that's just great.
Time to cut my losses. But I could use a diversion so I can slip out...
Say...
I'm such a genius, sometimes it frightens me.
Spider-Woman to Chameleon!
I am proceeding to our rendezvous point! We'll link up there and carry our loot out together!
Huh? Spider-Woman is... working with the Chameleon?
I thought she was on the side of the angels!
She's always been something of a dark angel.
Maybe she's gone so far over to the other side she can't find her way back.

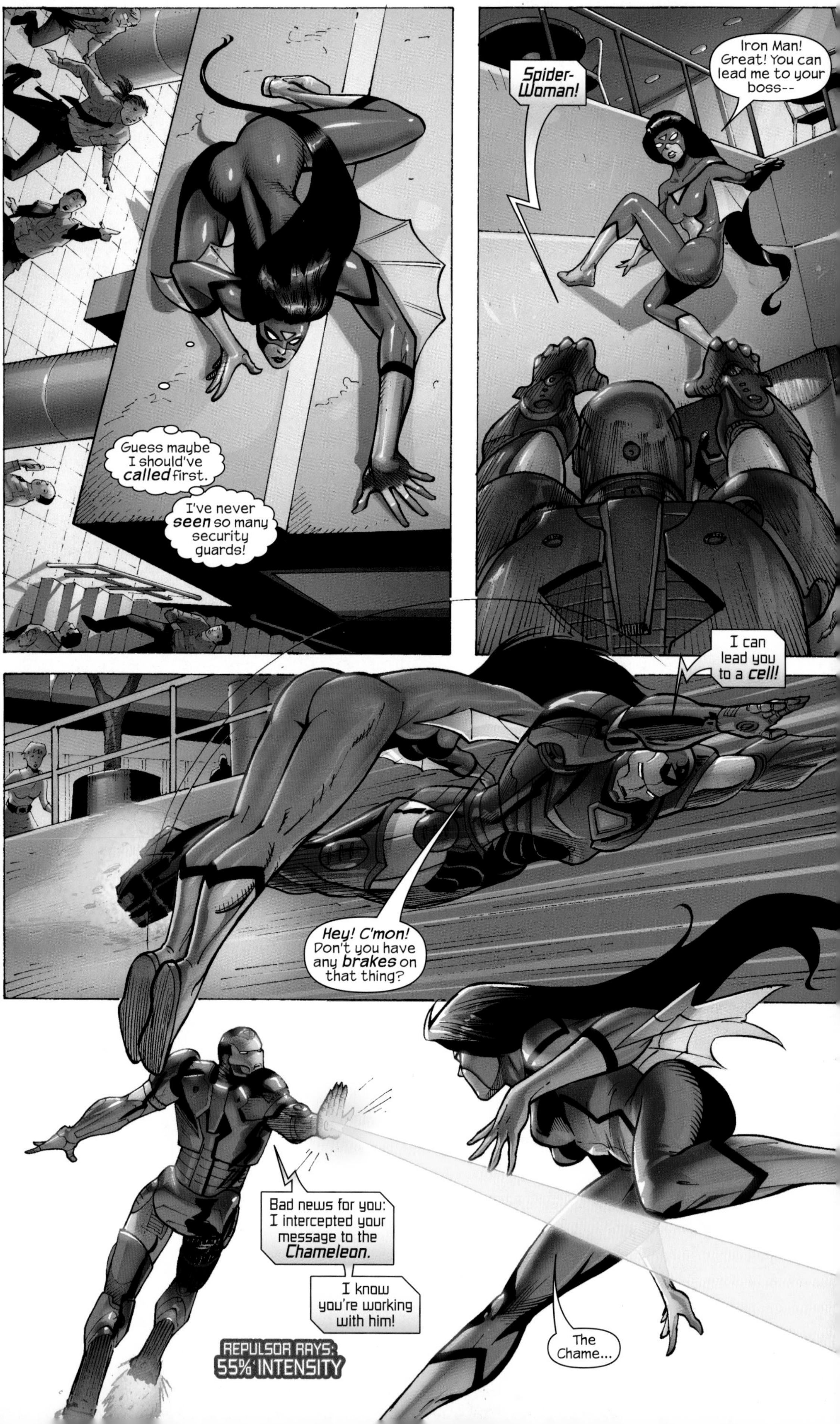

Guess maybe I should've called first.
I've never seen so many security guards!
Spider-Woman!
Iron Man! Great! You can lead me to your boss--
I can lead you to a cell!
Hey! C'mon! Don't you have any brakes on that thing?
Bad news for you: I intercepted your message to the Chameleon.
I know you're working with him!
REPULSOR RAYS: 55% INTENSITY
The Chame...

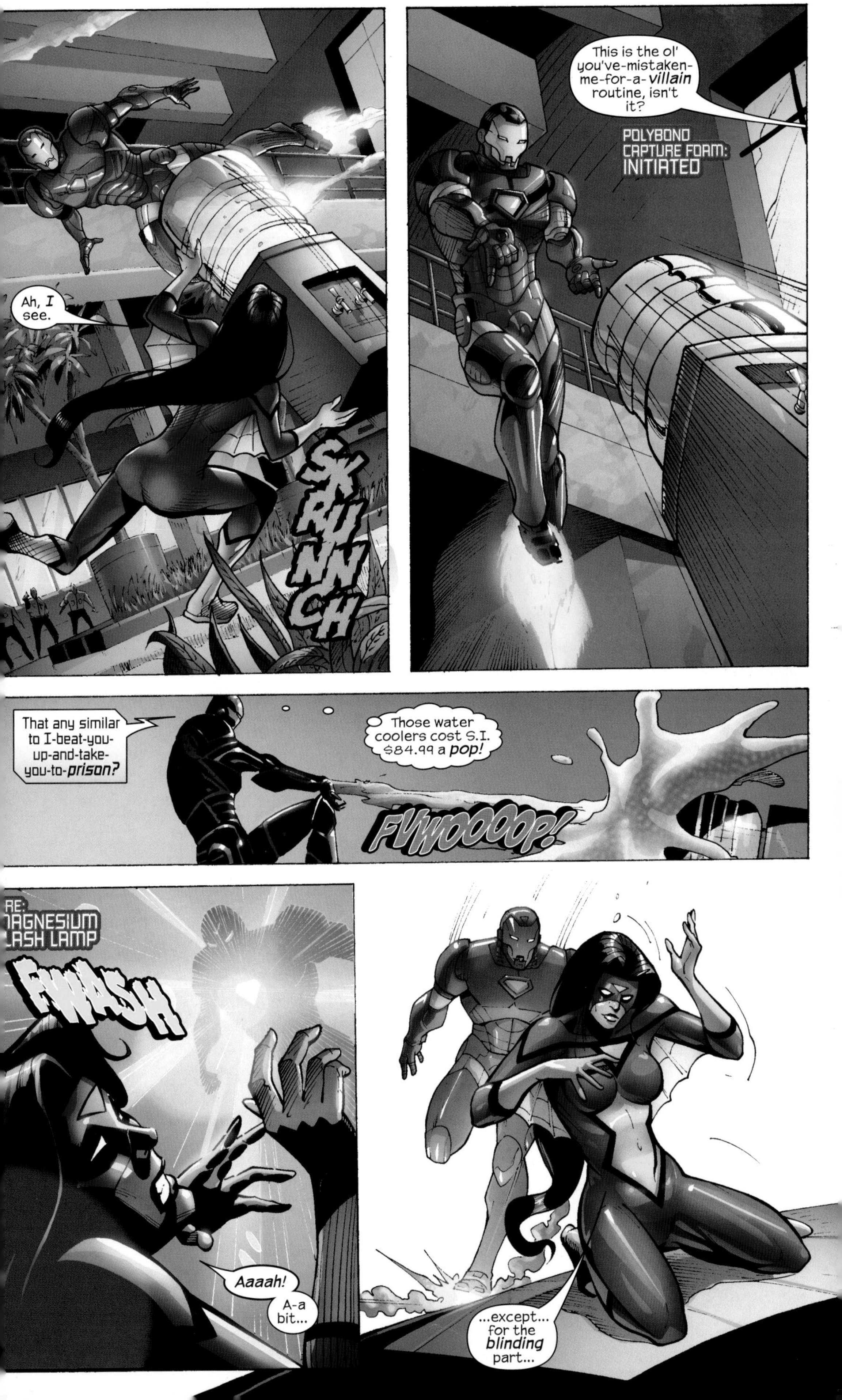
Ah, I see.
SKRUNNCH
This is the ol' you've-mistaken-me-for-a-villain routine, isn't it?
POLYBOND CAPTURE FORM: INITIATED
That any similar to I-beat-you-up-and-take-you-to-prison?
Those water coolers cost S.I. $84.99 a pop!
FVWOOOOP!
RE: AGNESIUM LASH LAMP
FWASH
Aaaah!
A-a bit...
...except... for the blinding part...

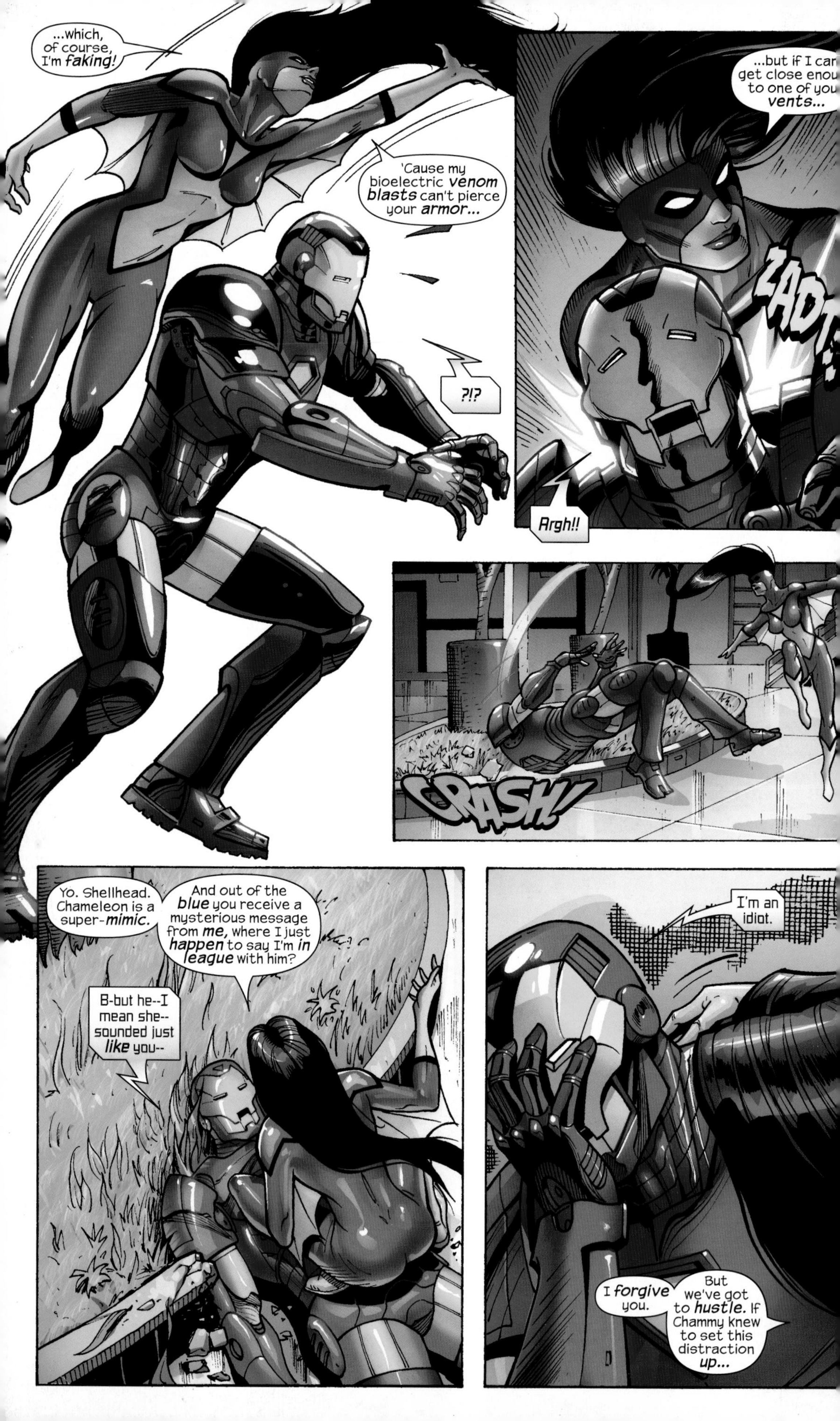

...which, of course, I'm faking!
'Cause my bioelectric venom blasts can't pierce your armor...
?!?
...but if I can get close enou to one of you vents...
ZADT
Argh!!
CRASH!
Yo. Shellhead. Chameleon is a super-mimic.
And out of the blue you receive a mysterious message from me, where I just happen to say I'm in league with him?
B-but he--I mean she--sounded just like you--
I'm an idiot.
I forgive you.
But we've got to hustle. If Chammy knew to set this distraction up...

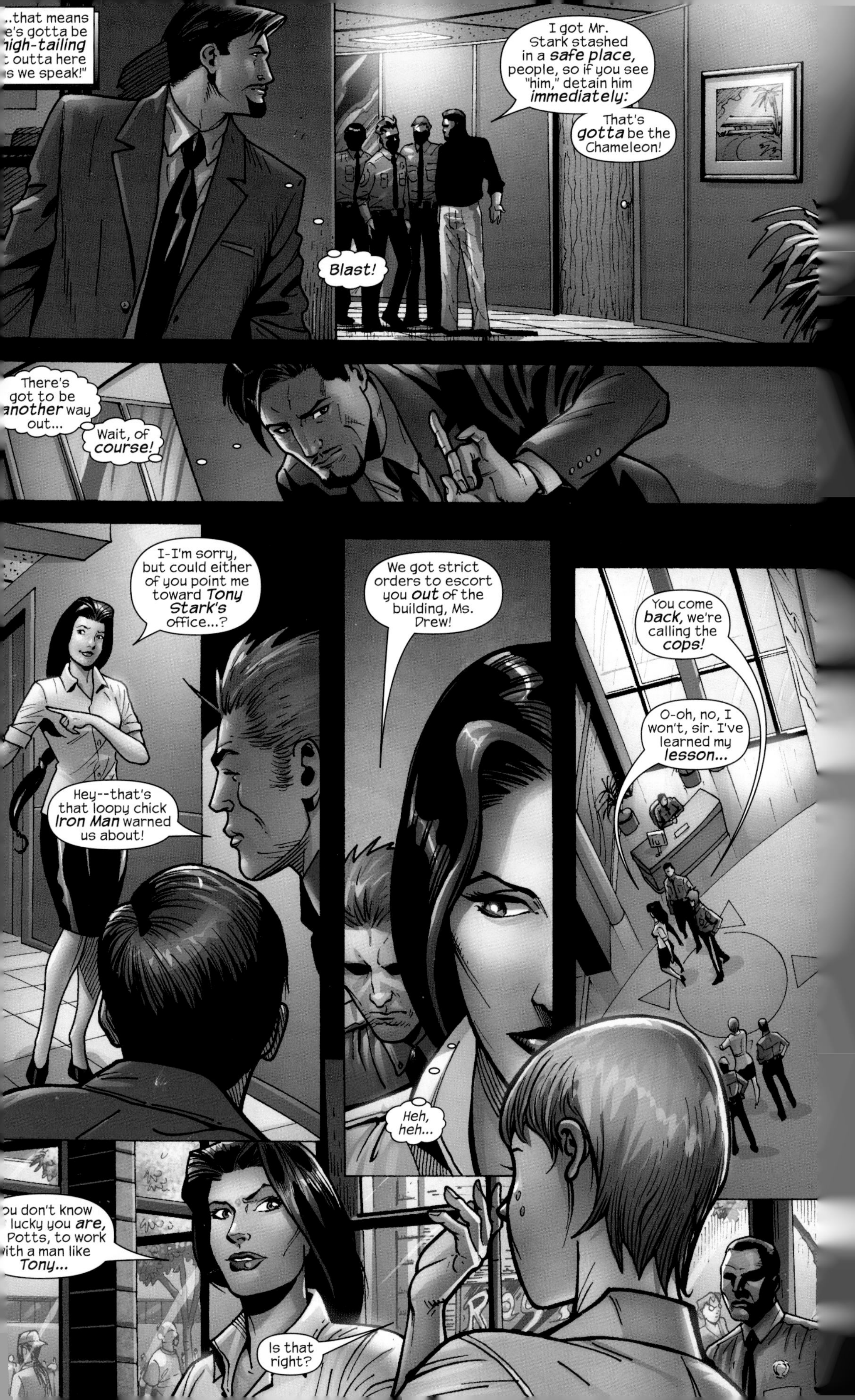

..that means
e's gotta be
high-tailing
outta here
s we speak!"
I got Mr. Stark stashed in a safe place, people, so if you see "him," detain him immediately:
That's gotta be the Chameleon!
Blast!
There's got to be another way out...
Wait, of course!
I-I'm sorry, but could either of you point me toward Tony Stark's office...?
Hey--that's that loopy chick Iron Man warned us about!
We got strict orders to escort you out of the building, Ms. Drew!
You come back, we're calling the cops!
O-oh, no, I won't, sir. I've learned my lesson...
Heh, heh...
ou don't know
lucky you are,
Potts, to work
ith a man like
Tony...
Is that right?

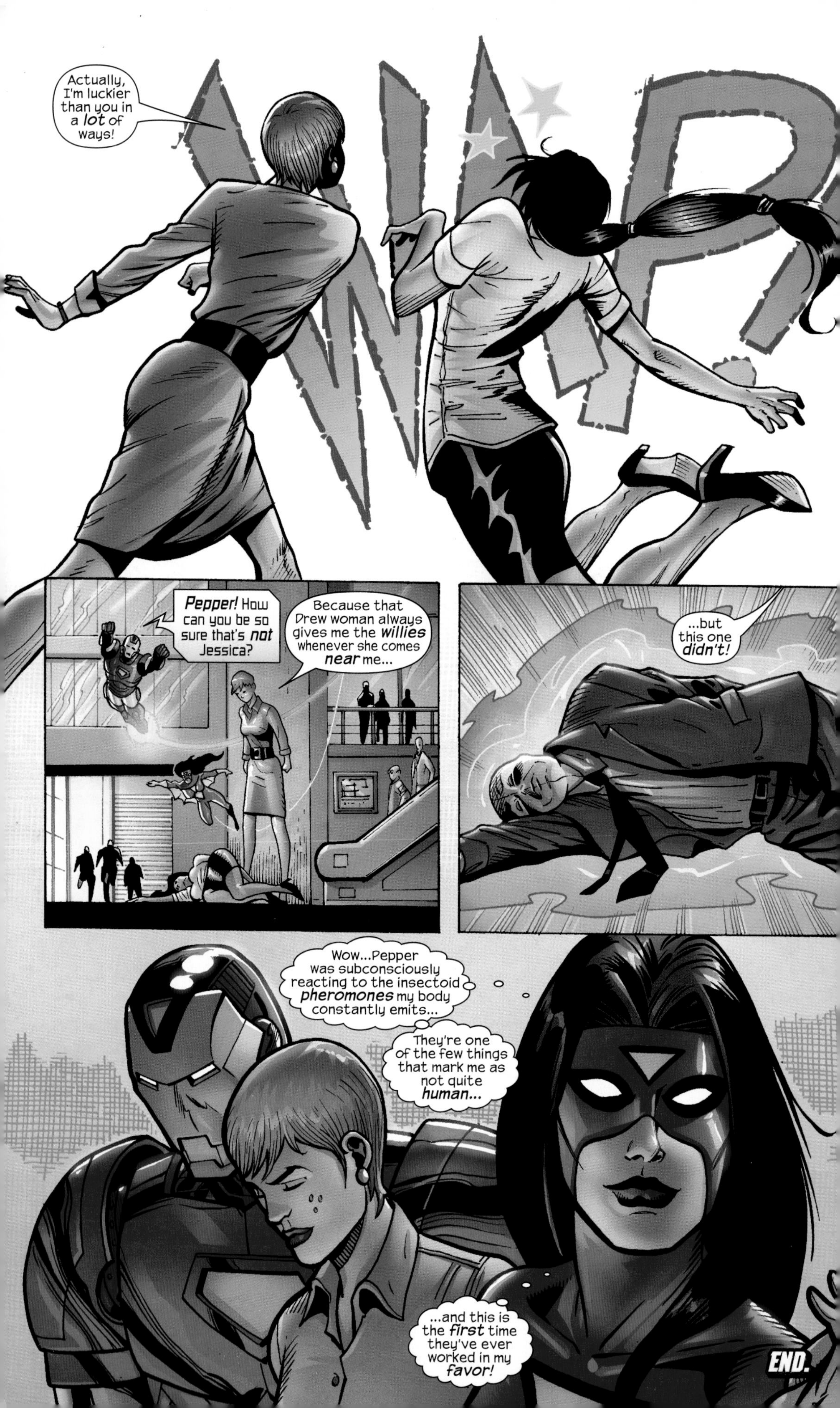
Actually, I'm luckier than you in a lot of ways!
Pepper! How can you be so sure that's not Jessica?
Because that Drew woman always gives me the willies whenever she comes near me...
...but this one didn't!
Wow...Pepper was subconsciously reacting to the insectoid pheromones my body constantly emits...
They're one of the few things that mark me as not quite human...
...and this is the first time they've ever worked in my favor!
END.